Presented to
Belmont Day School

by _____

date _____

Story by Jeffrey Allen
Pictures by James Marshall

Little, Brown and Company

BOSTON   TORONTO

Also by Jeffrey Allen and James Marshall:
Mary Alice, Operator Number Nine

First Edition

Library of Congress Cataloging-in-Publication Data
Allen, Jeffrey.
    Mary Alice returns.

    Summary: Mary Alice, the duck who is an efficient and con-
scientious telephone operator, attempts to track down an anony-
mous caller in distress.
    [1. Telephone—Fiction.   2. Ducks—Fiction]
I. Marshall, James, 1942–   ill.   II. Title.
PZ7.A4272Mas   1986   [E]   85-23064
ISBN 0-316-03429-0

WOR

*Published simultaneously in Canada
by Little, Brown & Company (Canada) Limited*

Printed in the United States of America

FOR JOHN KELLER

"At the sound of the tone,
the time will be three o'clock, exactly. Quack!
At the sound of the tone,
the time will be three o'clock and five seconds. Quack!
At the sound of the tone,
the time will be three o'clock and ten seconds. Quack!"
Mary Alice, Operator Number Nine, was at her
switchboard.
She enjoyed what she did best —
giving the precise time.
"At the sound of the tone,
the time will be three o'clock and twenty-five seconds.
Quack!"

Everyone in town loved Mary Alice.
"She's so good at her job," people would say.
"We can always rely on Mary Alice to give us the correct time."

Then one day, something peculiar happened.
Mary Alice was announcing the time
when suddenly she heard
"Help!…Help!" over her headphone.
She listened carefully.
"Help!…Help!" the voice repeated.
"Who *is* this?" Mary Alice asked.
But there was no reply.

"This is terrible!" Mary Alice said.
"What if someone was in an avalanche or
is lost in the desert? Maybe someone
fell off a train. I'd better tell Boss Chicken."

"You're working too hard, and just imagining things,"
Boss Chicken told Mary Alice. "Your job does get monotonous."
But Mary Alice was certain that she had heard a cry for help.

Mary Alice was upset,
and returned to her switchboard.
"At the sound of the tone,
the time will be five-fifteen and ten seconds. Quack!
At the sound of the tone,
the time will be five-fifteen and fifteen seconds. Quack!
At the sound of the…"
"Help!…Help!"
The voice was back!
Mary Alice ran to get Boss Chicken, who
listened in.
"You're right!" Boss Chicken said.
"This *is* terrible!"

Mary Alice went to the police to find out
if they had received any unusual calls for help.
"Just four burglaries, two car crashes, and
a Mr. Charlie Armadillo reported that
his spectacles were stolen," the inspector said.

Mary Alice then hurried over to the
fire department.
"It's been pretty quiet around here,"
said the chief.

Mary Alice decided to place
a personal advertisement in the newspaper.
It read: "Will the person who keeps calling me
for help please call back? I care. Signed,
Mary Alice, Operator Number Nine."

Mary Alice also rented a biplane.
She flew over town pulling a sign:
"If you need help, call Mary Alice,
Operator Number Nine."

Mary Alice received many calls for help—
but not the one she expected.
"Is it safe to keep a tuna casserole
in the refrigerator for more than two weeks?"
Mrs. Johnson wanted to know.

"I'm traveling to Calcutta in December," said Eric Snake. "Should I pack a sweater?"

Mary Alice was getting anxious.
She moved her bed next to the switchboard
so she wouldn't miss a single call.
Boss Chicken brought in coffee
and doughnuts.

All day and night, Mary Alice continued
to give the correct time.
"At the sound of the tone,
the time will be four-thirteen and five seconds. Quack!
At the sound of the tone,
the time will be four-thirteen and ten seconds. Quack!
At the sound of the tone,
the time will be four-thirteen and…"
"Help!…Help!"
This time Mary Alice was prepared.

In a flash, she put on her hard hat,
climbed a telephone pole,
and hooked up a special line.
"The call is coming from 15 Gardenia Street!"
Mary Alice shouted down to
Boss Chicken.

Mary Alice and Boss Chicken
rushed over to the house on Gardenia Street.
They looked in the window.
"Ah ha!" cried Boss Chicken.

Karen Squirrel was putting her doll
up against the telephone.
"Help!…Help!"
the doll cried.

Mary Alice and Boss Chicken went in,
took the doll away from Karen Squirrel,
and hung up the telephone.

"I was just playing," Karen Squirrel said.
"We don't play with the telephone company,"
Boss Chicken said in her most serious voice.
"Do you know how worried we were?" Mary Alice asked.
Karen Squirrel suddenly realized what she had done,
and all the trouble she had caused.
"I'm sorry, Mary Alice," she said.

Mary Alice was glad that nobody
was in danger. She took Karen Squirrel
to the amusement park. The roller coaster
nearly scared their socks off.

But the biggest thrill for Karen Squirrel
was being able to sit at Mary Alice's switchboard.
She was even given a set of headphones.
"At the sound of the tone…"

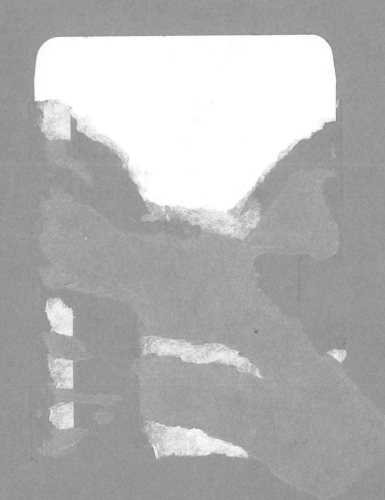

INSECTS

© 1993 Franklin Watts

Franklin Watts, Inc.
95 Madison Avenue
New York, NY 10016

10 9 8 7 6 5 4 3 2 1

Library of Congress Cataloging-in-Publication Data

Richardson, Joy.
    Insects / by Joy Richardson.
        p. cm — (Picture science)
    Includes index.
    Summary: A simple introduction to the physical characteristics and
life cycle of insects.
    ISBN 0-531-14248-5
    1. Insects—Juvenile literature. [1. Insects.] I. Title.
  II. Series: Richardson, Joy. Picture science.
QL467.2.R53 1993
595.7—dc20   92-32189
                                           CIP AC

Editor: Sarah Ridley
Designer: Janet Watson
Picture researcher: Sarah Moule
Illustrator: Linda Costello

Photographs: Bruce Coleman 7, 9, 14, 16, 21;
Robert Harding Picture Library 19; Frank Lane
Picture Agency 13; Natural History
Photographic Agency cover, 10, 22, 25, 27.

Printed in Malaysia

PICTURE SCIENCE

INSECTS

Joy Richardson

FRANKLIN WATTS
New York ● Chicago ● London ● Toronto ● Sydney

Insects everywhere

The world is full of insects.
For every single person in the world
there are a hundred million insects.

There are hundreds of thousands
of different types of insect.

The world needs insects.
They can do a lot of damage,
but they do a lot of good, too.

Laying eggs

All insects start life inside an egg.

Female insects lay eggs
through tubes at the
back of their body.

Some insects glue their eggs
in place with sticky liquid.

Some insects drill
into leaves or seeds
to lay their eggs.

Some insects lay their eggs
in holes underground.

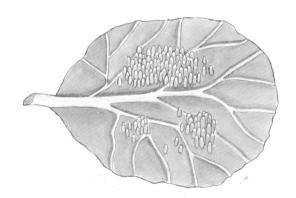

Starting life

A newborn insect is called a larva.
Most insect larvae are
nothing like their parents.

When a butterfly egg hatches,
a caterpillar crawls out.

The caterpillar feeds on plants.
It sheds its skin several times
as it grows longer and fatter.

When it is fully grown,
the caterpillar prepares
for a big change.

Changes

The caterpillar wraps itself up.
It spins a cocoon or forms
an outer case around itself.
It is now called a pupa.

It stays quite still while
its whole body changes.
Inside the pupa case,
legs and wings start growing.

Weeks later, a butterfly emerges.
The caterpillar has disappeared.

Growing up

Bees and wasps make nests.
The larvae live in special compartments
until they change into adults.

Stick insects hatch from their eggs
looking like tiny adults.
They just keep changing
their skins as they grow bigger.

Caddis fly larvae live underwater.
They make cases of stones and shells
to hide in while they grow their wings.

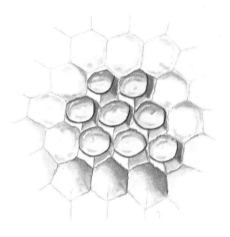

A skeleton on the outside

An insect has no bones.
Its skeleton is on the
outside of its body.

This skeleton is a casing of
tough skin called the cuticle.

All the muscles that
move the legs and wings
are attached to the
inside of the cuticle.

The cuticle protects the
insect's soft insides and
keeps it from drying out.

A body in three parts

Adult insects have three parts to their body.

The head is at the front.

The thorax is in the middle with legs and wings attached to it.

The abdomen is at the back. It is usually the biggest part.

Each part is made up of segments. This helps the body to bend.

Breathing

Insects do not breathe
through their mouths.
They take in air through holes
along the sides of their body.

Tubes from the air holes
branch out to every part of the body.

Oxygen from the air passes
into the muscles to make energy.

Lots of air goes to the thorax
where energy is needed
to drive the legs and wings.

Legs

All insects have six legs
attached to the thorax.

The legs bend at the joints
where the cuticle is very thin.

Insects are steady walkers.
They keep a triangle of
three legs on the ground
while they move the other three.

On the ends of their legs there are
tiny claws and sticky pads.
These help with walking upside down.

Wings

Most insects can fly.
They have one or two pairs of
wings attached to the thorax.

Muscles make the wings move.
Some flies can beat their wings
hundreds of times in a second.

Beetles hide their wings away.
When they fly, the front covers lift
and the back wings unfold.

Dragonflies keep their
wings spread out to glide
and swoop on smaller insects.

Heads

Insects have two large eyes
on the sides of their head.
The eyes are made up of
lots of little lenses.
Each lens catches a spot of light.

Insects can see all around.
They cannot see very clearly but
they can spot the smallest movements.

Insects have antennae
on the front of their head.
Antennae collect information
about touch and taste
and sounds and smells.

Real insects

Not all creepy crawly creatures are insects, though they may have a lot in common.

Worms and wood lice, centipedes, and spiders are not real insects.

All insects lay eggs.
They have skeletons on the outside.
Their bodies have three parts with segments.
They have air holes in their sides.
They have six legs attached to the thorax.
Their eyes are made up of many little eyes.
They have antennae on their head.

Index